To my
Valentine

Miss Flora Mc Flimsey's
Valentine

THE NINE FLORA McFLIMSEY BOOKS

Miss Flora McFlimsey's
Valentine

BY MARIANA

Lothrop, Lee & Shepard Books   *New York*

ILLUSTRATIONS BY MARIANA RECREATED BY CAROLINE WALTON HOWE.

Copyright © 1962 by Lothrop, Lee & Shepard Co. Inc., 1987 by Erik Bjork.
All rights reserved. No part of this book may be reproduced or utilized in any form or by any means, electronic or mechanical, including photocopying, recording or by any information storage and retrieval system, without permission in writing from the Publisher. Inquiries should be addressed to Lothrop, Lee & Shepard Books, a division of William Morrow & Company, Inc., 105 Madison Avenue, New York, New York 10016. Printed in the United States of America.

First Edition 1 2 3 4 5 6 7 8 9 10

Library of Congress Cataloging in Publication Data
Mariana.   Miss Flora McFlimsey's valentine.
Summary: Miss Flora McFlimsey makes and sends surprise cards to her friends for Valentine's Day, although her lazy cat Pookoo almost causes her plans to fail. [1. Valentine's Day—Fiction. 2. Dolls—Fiction] I. Title. PZ7.M33825Mm 1987 [E] 86-15254
ISBN 0-688-04547-2   ISBN 0-688-04548-0 (lib. bdg.)

One winter evening Miss Flora McFlimsey and Pookoo
Cat were sitting before the fireplace in the dollhouse.

"Mr. Pookoo," said Miss Flora McFlimsey, "did you
ever get a valentine?"

"What's that?" asked Pookoo.

I love You

"It's something that has lace on it and a heart and flowers and white birds, and it says 'I Love You,' and nobody knows who sends it."

"Then nobody gets thanked," said Pookoo. "What's the use of giving something that you don't get thanked for?"

Miss Flora McFlimsey did not answer. She was remembering that once long ago she had seen a valentine.

The little girl who owned her then had held her in her arms and let her look at it. It smelled like violets, and it said: "To my dearest love."

The little girl had explained that valentines only came on the fourteenth day of February. But all that was long ago.

"Mr. Pookoo," said Miss Flora McFlimsey suddenly, "what's today?"

Pookoo counted on his toes. "It's Friday, February thirteenth."

"Then tomorrow," said Miss Flora McFlimsey, "is Valentine's Day." She thought a moment. "It would be nice to send a valentine to Timothy Mouse."

"Why to Timothy Mouse?" asked Pookoo.

"Because he is so little. Perhaps no one else will think about him."

"*I* think about him quite often," remarked Pookoo.

Miss Flora McFlimsey hastily changed the subject.

"And Oliver Owl must be lonely up in that hollow tree."

"Nonsense!" said Pookoo. "His nephew lives with him. Besides, if he were as wise as he thinks he is, he'd be living in a nice warm barn, not in that hollow tree."

"And Tuffy Puffin," said Miss Flora. "I don't suppose anyone ever sent him a valentine."

"Do you mean that old bird who lives in the big rocks? He doesn't deserve a valentine. Every time I go near there he gives me a peck on the head."

"And Peterkins," said Miss Flora McFlimsey. "He must get tired of that burrow he lives in all winter."

"Just wait till spring," said Pookoo. "He'll be hopping about as sassy as ever. But really, Miss McFlimsey, why don't you go to bed and stop thinking about such foolishness?"

Pookoo Cat yawned and stretched himself out on the hearth rug. Miss Flora McFlimsey waited until he was asleep. Then she tiptoed over to her little trunk in the corner.

She stood on top of it and took down from the shelf the
little girl's scissors and colored pencils and bottle of paste
and writing paper.

She opened the trunk and snipped some lace off her best
petticoat and cut some forget-me-nots and ribbons from
her summer hat.

Then she made a valentine

for Tuffy Puffin

and one for Oliver Owl

and one for Peterkins

and a very tiny one for Timothy Mouse.

She put them all in her little basket and carried it over to Pookoo. She rang the bell on his collar three times. Pookoo didn't stir.

"Mr. Pookoo Cat," she said, "will you be so kind as to carry my valentines? You walk so softly, and nobody can see you in the dark. So no one will know who sent them."

Pookoo began to snore.

Miss Flora McFlimsey whispered in his ear. "Mr. Pookoo Cat, would you like me to get you some catnip from the cupboard?"

Pookoo sat up. "A big bunch?" he asked.

"As much as I can carry."

Miss Flora hurriedly took off Pookoo's little bell and fastened the basket to his collar, talking all the while. "Please leave this one for Peterkins at his burrow, and Oliver Owl's at the hollow tree, and Timothy Mouse's at his little hole, and Tuffy Puffin's down by the big rocks."

She opened the door and Pookoo disappeared into the night.

Miss Flora McFlimsey got the catnip. "I'll warm some milk for him too, and have it ready when he gets back," she said.

Then she sat in her rocking chair and waited.

After a long while there was a scratching at the door. In walked Pookoo. He seemed very pleased with himself. "All went well," he announced, brushing the snow off his coat.

"Where's the catnip?"

Miss Flora McFlimsey poured his warm milk. He lapped it up and nipped the catnip. Then he lay down in front of the fire and was soon sound asleep.

"Now I can sleep too," thought Miss Flora McFlimsey happily.

But a moment later she remembered. There was no valentine for Pookoo! How could she have forgotten him? He had been such a good, kind cat to carry her valentines out on a cold night.

She hurried to get another piece of paper. She drew a big heart and wrote on it "To one I love." She tied it with her blue hair ribbon, and she laid it beside his saucer where he would see it the first thing in the morning.

TO ONE love I LOVE MY VALEN TIN E

"Now I can really go to sleep," she said. But just at that moment there came a tap-tap on the windowpane. Two round green eyes were peering in. Miss Flora McFlimsey opened the window. It was little Oscar Owlet. He seemed very excited.

"Hoot, Miss McFlimsey," he said. "I have a message for you from Uncle Oliver Owl. He sends you his compliments and says to tell you what that rascal of a Pookoo Cat did. He stuffed all your valentines into our hollow tree and ran off down the lane!"

"But don't cry, Miss McFlimsey," he added quickly. "As you know, my uncle is a very wise bird and he has a plan. Now listen carefully. Uncle Oliver will open a post office in our hollow tree. You are to make a sign to pin on it. I am to fly quickly before daylight to each one of your friends and tell them to come at once to the post office for an important letter."

"Oh, Pookoo! How could you?" Miss Flora McFlimsey scolded.

Pookoo opened one eye, then closed it quickly.

Miss Flora McFlimsey was already
making a sign.

"Very good," said Oscar Owlet, who
had flown in and lighted on her shoulder
in a friendly sort of way.

Miss Flora McFlimsey looked
at Pookoo. He seemed to be
sleeping peacefully. She
hesitated just a moment, then
she picked up the valentine
she had made for him.

"Take this too," she said.

Oscar Owlet was gone with
a flutter, and in two winks
Miss Flora McFlimsey was
asleep.

It was broad daylight when
she opened her eyes. The
window was still open, and
Pookoo Cat was gone.

"Hoot, hoot." A little ball of feathers lit on the window-sill. It was Oscar Owlet again.

"Hurry, Miss McFlimsey," he said. "The post office is open and all is ready. Uncle Oliver says you are to follow me to the big apple tree and hide behind it. You can watch from there and see everything that happens."

Miss Flora McFlimsey put on her hat and velvet cape and fur-lined boots and her ermine muff and white kid gloves.

Oscar Owlet flew just ahead of her.

They passed Peterkins coming out of his burrow on his way to the post office.
But they pretended not to see him.

When they reached the apple tree, Oscar Owlet perched on a top branch. Miss Flora McFlimsey hid carefully behind it.

She could see the hollow tree down the road with
Oliver Owl sitting inside.

First came Tuffy Puffin. He looked at his valentine sideways, then upside down. Then he flew around it twice and lit on top of it, chirping all the while:

"Now *who* could have sent it! It *might* have been Miss Pigeon. It *might* have been Miss Penguin," until Oliver Owl called out, "Don't block the line!" Then off he flew with the valentine, still chirping, "Now it just *might* have been Miss Sea Gull..."

Next came Timothy Mouse. He clutched his tiny valentine in his paws and scurried off.

Peterkins' ears were wiggling with excitement as he came up to the hollow tree. "Goodbye, Mr. Owl!" he cried. He always got things mixed up and said goodbye when he meant to say hello. He hopped off with his valentine calling, "Hello, Mr. Owl." Of course he meant goodbye.

Last in line, and walking softly on his velvety paws, came Pookoo. He padded gracefully up to the hollow tree. "Is there anything for me?" he purred.

Oliver Owl handed him a little roll of paper tied with a blue ribbon.

Pookoo bounded away with it toward the old apple tree.

"It's the prettiest of all," he purred proudly.

Then he caught sight of Miss Flora McFlimsey peeping out from behind the tree, and he felt just a little ashamed.

But Miss Flora McFlimsey wasn't thinking about him at all. She was watching an elderly rabbit, wearing an odd sort of hat, hopping slowly along the path.

It was Peterkins' aunt! Miss Flora ran down the path to meet her.

"I'm on my way to the post office," explained Peterkins' aunt politely. "Peterkins thought there might be a valentine for me, too."

Oh! thought Miss Flora McFlimsey. Why didn't I make just one more!

And she remembered the beautiful Easter bonnet Peterkins' aunt had once made for her.

Pookoo had been listening, and he knew how bad Miss Flora must be feeling because there was no valentine for Peterkins' aunt. Then he had an idea.

"Oh, Mrs. Cottontail," he said. "Oliver Owl saw you coming and asked me to give this to you." And he dropped his own valentine at her feet.

"Why, thank you, Pookoo," said Peterkins' aunt. "What a pretty blue ribbon! I can use it to trim a hat."

Miss Flora McFlimsey and Pookoo walked home together.

"That was nice of you, Pookoo," said Miss Flora McFlimsey, as she opened the door of the dollhouse. Then she gave a little cry of surprise. For there, slipped under the door, was a large white envelope sealed with a red heart. It said *For Miss Flora McFlimsey.*

She opened it quickly and read...
Roses are red
Violets are blue
Miss Flora, I love you
Your true friend—Pookoo

"Oh! It's just beautiful!" cried Miss Flora McFlimsey. Pookoo purred.